A LETTER TO AMY

For Augusta Baker

A LETTER TO AMY. Copyright © 1968 by Ezra Jack Keats.
Printed in the United States of America. All rights reserved.
Library of Congress Catalog Card Number: 68–24329.
ISBN 0-06-023108-4
ISBN 0-06-023109-2 (lib. bdg.)

U.S. MAIL

USE ZIP CODE
NUMBERS

MAIL EARLY IN THE DAY

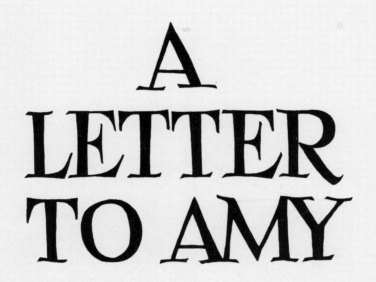

EZRA JACK KEATS

A
LETTER
TO AMY

■ HarperCollins*Publishers*

"I'm writing a letter to Amy.

I'm inviting her to my party," Peter announced.

"Why don't you just ask her? You didn't write

to anyone else," said his mother.

Peter stared at the sheet of paper for a while and said,

"We-e-el-l, this way it's sort of special."

He folded the letter quite a few times,
put it in the envelope, and sealed it.
"Now I'll mail it," he said.
"What did you write?" his mother asked.
WILL YOU PLEASE COME
TO MY BIRTHDAY PARTY. PETER.
"You should tell her when to come."
So he wrote on the back of the envelope:
IT IS THIS SATURDAY AT 2.
"Now I'll mail it."
"Put on a stamp."
He did, and started to leave.
"Wear your raincoat. It looks like rain."
He put it on and said, "It looks like rain.
You'd better stay in, Willie,"
and ran out to mail his letter.

Walking to the mailbox, Peter looked at the sky.
Dark clouds raced across it like wild horses.
He glanced up at Amy's window. She wasn't there.
Only Pepe, her parrot, sat peering down.
"Willie! Didn't I tell you to stay home?"

It is this Saturday at 2.

Peter thought, What will the boys say
when they see a girl at my party?
Suddenly there was a flash of lightning
and a roar of thunder!
A strong wind blew the letter out of his hand!

Peter chased the letter.
He tried to stop it with his foot, but it blew away.

Then it flew high into the air—

and landed, skipping across a hopscotch game.

The letter blew this way and that.
Peter chased it this way and that.
He couldn't catch it.

Big drops of rain began to fall.
Just then someone turned the corner.
It was Amy! She waved to him.
The letter flew right toward her.

She mustn't see it, or the surprise will be spoiled!
They both ran for the letter.

In his great hurry, Peter bumped into Amy.
He caught the letter before she could see it was for her.

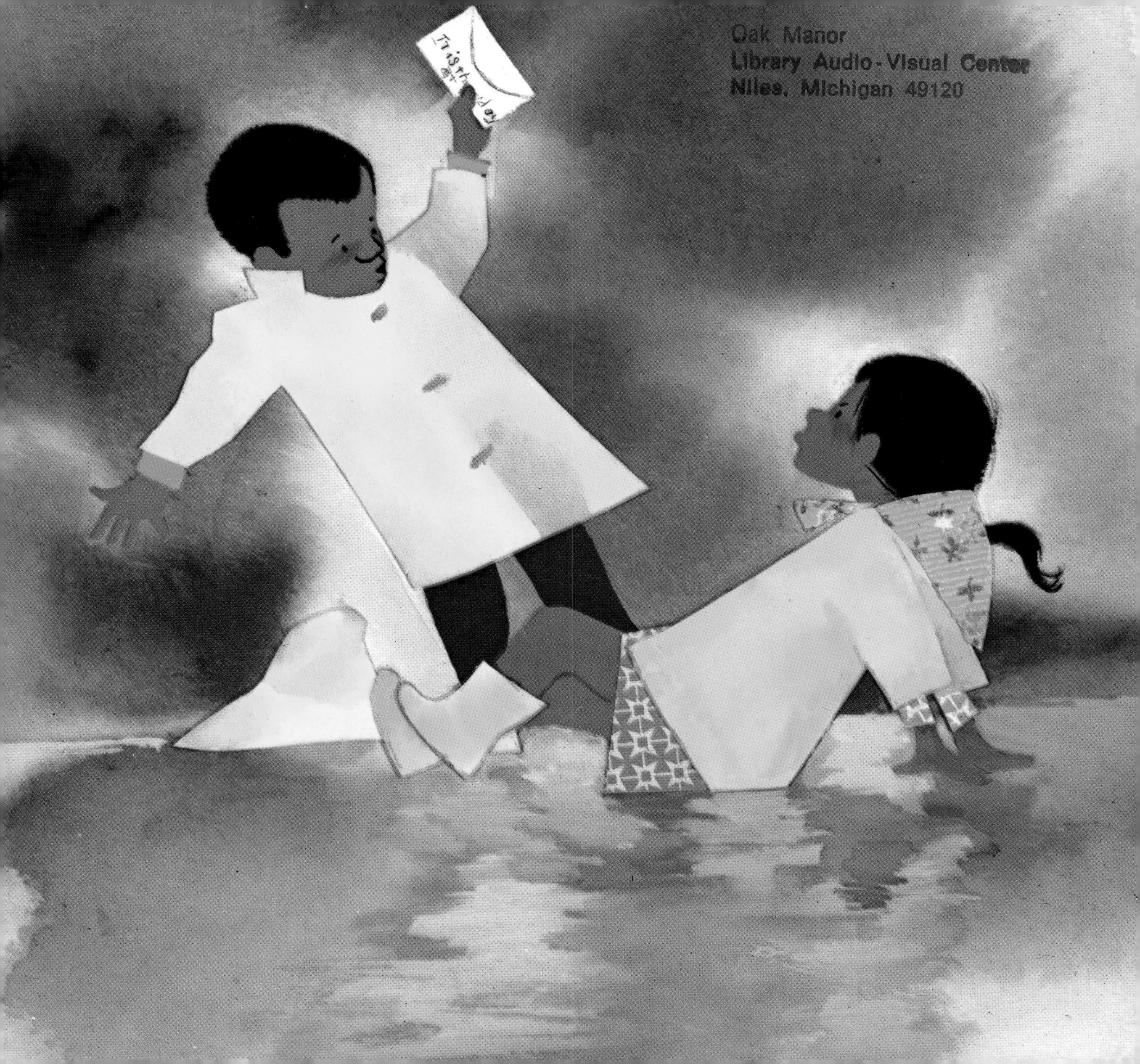

Quickly he stuffed the letter into the mailbox.
He looked for Amy, but she had run off crying.

Now she'll never come to my party, thought Peter.
He saw his reflection in the street.
It looked all mixed up.

When Peter got back to his house, his mother asked, "Did you mail your letter?"

"Yes," he said sadly.

Saturday came at last.
Everybody arrived but Amy.

"Shall I bring the cake out now?" his mother asked Peter.

"Let's wait a little," said Peter.

"Now! Bring it out now!" chanted the boys.

"All right," said Peter slowly, "bring it out now."

Just then the door opened.
In walked Amy with her parrot!
"A girl—ugh!" said Eddie.

"Happy Birthday, Peter!" said Amy.
"HAAPPY BIRRRTHDAY, PEEETERRR!"
repeated the parrot.

Peter's mother brought in the cake she had baked
and lit the candles. Everyone sang.
"Make a wish!" cried Amy.
"Wish for a truck full of ice cream!" shouted Eddie.
"A store full of candy and no stomach-ache!"

But Peter made his own wish,
and blew out all the candles at once.

Ezra Jack Keats was born in Brooklyn, and lived all his life in New York except for Army service in World War II and, later, a year of travel and study abroad, mostly in Paris. In 1963 Mr. Keats was awarded the Caldecott Medal for his book THE SNOWY DAY. He is the author and illustrator of many other classic books for children, among them WHISTLE FOR WILLIE, JOHN HENRY, GOD IS IN THE MOUNTAIN, JENNIE'S HAT, and PETER'S CHAIR.